fr: Jocelyn

SOMEBODY SOMEWHERE
Knows My Name

by Linda Lowery
illustrated by John Eric Karpinski

Carolrhoda Books, Inc./Minneapolis

Many thanks to everyone who supported this project, especially: Jill Anderson for her profound understanding of the creative process; Emily Kelley, John Swanholm, Bob Strachota, and Paul Howey for orchestrating it all; Lori Lowery, Kerry MacLean, and Judith Fisher for helping me keep the story true to my heart; Joan Jendro, Monsignor Boxleitner, and the St. Joseph's intake staff for making my job easier; and JoEllen Hall for letting me borrow her name.

—L.L.

Special thanks to Jennie Birenbaum, Jeff Carlson, and Chandra Small for serving as models for the artist.

This book is a joint project of Carolrhoda Books, Inc., and St. Joseph's Home for Children, Minneapolis, Minnesota.

Carolrhoda Books, Inc. c/o The Lerner Group
241 First Avenue North, Minneapolis, MN 55401

LIBRARY OF CONGRESS CATALOGING-IN-PUBLICATION DATA
Lowery, Linda.
   Somebody somewhere knows my name / by Linda Lowery ; illustrated by John Eric Karpinski.
   p. cm.
   Summary: Grace describes what happens when she and her little brother are abandoned by their mother and stay at an emergency shelter for children.
   ISBN 0-87614-946-8 (lib. bdg.)
   [1. Abandoned children—Fiction. 2. Brothers and sisters—Fiction.]
I. Karpinski, John Eric, ill. II. Title.
PZ7.L9653So 1995
[Fic]—dc20   94-49538
                                                                    CIP
                                                                     AC

Manufactured in the United States of America
1 2 3 4 5 6 – JR – 00 99 98 97 96 95

To the wonderful kids
passing through St. Joe's while I was there—
my heart will remember each of you,
no matter how much time goes by.

I hear the car door slam loud, like a firecracker in a tin can. Like a shot. Even though I am closed up in the gas station bathroom, I hear it. I zip up my pants and race outside.

The tail lights speed off like mean red eyes. Then there's nothing.

No sound.

No dust.

Nothing.

She left a paper bag behind, the one our clothes are in. It's sitting on the edge of the road, rattling in the wind.

My blood feels thin, like it's draining from my veins. This must be how you feel when you've been shot and all your blood is leaving your body, and soon there's nothing left and you just disappear.

Not a trace left behind.

When Willy comes out of the boys' bathroom, he strolls toward me like a tough guy, even though he's only eight. I can't watch him smiling at me. More than anything in the world, I want to tell him a big fat lie about how Mom went to the store to buy us Chunky Monkey. It's our favorite name of ice cream, but she never had enough money to buy it for us. "Mom's coming back with Chunky Monkey," I want to tell him.

Instead, I sit down in the dust. "We'll just wait here a while," I say.

He asks me a bunch of questions, but I don't answer. I just look down at the ground. When Willy finally gets quiet, I look in his eyes. I know he knows and he knows I know, but neither of us says it out loud.

So we wait here, writing with our fingers in the gravel. *M-O-M*, Willy writes. Then *m-o-m*, curly-like. I know what he's thinking. Writing it will bring her back. It's a magic thing.

Even though I know better, I write it too: *M-O-M*, with a heart around it. Maybe that

will send her a silent message that I love her. I'm sure she doesn't know it. I'm usually talking about other things, like jeans and haircuts she can't afford.

She never liked me asking for all those things. Actually, she never liked me much, period.

I concentrate on Willy's head, curl after curl, because I don't want to look around. If I look, I might see something terrible. Like a wild dog. Or nothing at all.

If I don't look, I can imagine I hear wheels crunching on the gravel, slowing down when they come near us, a door opening, me and Willy hopping in.

It's too dark to dust-write anymore. It isn't working anyway. She's not coming back.

The wind has picked up, and there's grit in my teeth. Willy is shivering, silent. I make him put on my sweatshirt. I move closer to keep the wind and the dirt from hitting him, and then curl up, clutching the brown bag to my chest so no one can stab me in the heart. Not that it would matter to me. But it would to Willy. Then who would he have to keep the grit out of his eyes?

The police bring us to a place where they take kids who get left. A man in a ponytail talks to us real soft. He asks my name. I don't say.

My mother calls me "girl," or "you." Sometimes she calls me "will you," as in "Get me a beer, *will you?*" I guess it was my father who gave me my real name. She must hate that.

"I'm nobody," I want to tell this man, "so quit asking." But that would sound stupid. So I keep my words inside, way down.

Willy takes his cues from me. He doesn't move, he doesn't speak. I make sure the ponytail guy doesn't touch him. He knows better than to touch me, because I've given him my evil eye.

It goes OK. He doesn't touch us, he doesn't get mad at us, he doesn't ask us about our names again.

Good thing for him.

We get showers and warm clothes. Then we go into a room where other kids are. It's kind of like kindergarten. There are bright lights and long, clean tables. Scribbly drawings are taped on the walls, made by kids who were here before us.

The lady in charge is JoEllen. She acts like she's our aunt and we've come for Thanksgiving dinner. "How about some apple juice?" she says.

Me and Willy give each other a look. It's the look that says we like her.

Everybody's sitting around painting pictures. I paint myself with a blue head and long red fingers. I'm having a problem with the mouth. I want to make it wide open, with fangs. But then some busybody will want to talk to me about it. Instead, I skip it. No mouth.

On the wall next to me is a poster of a big lady sunk in an armchair with three kids climbing all over her. She's smiling, and the kids are making dents in her soft body, and she doesn't even push them off. I don't think Willy should have to see that. Why should those kids get what he can't have?

"Your foster mother is here for you," someone tells the girl beside me. She's shiny and pretty, with a sky-blue hair ribbon. I'm sure she wasn't left at a gas station. I bet she's going to a house with a dog and daffodils and soft chairs and a room of her own.

Everybody tells her good-bye. JoEllen gives her a hug.

I turn away. I dip my brush in every color, dip, dip, dip, till they all turn brown. I paint brown streaks across my painting, across my blue face, across my red fingers. For a minute I feel better. But then I look around at everybody else's paintings, and mine looks dumb.

JoEllen doesn't make a stink. She just washes off the paints. Every color is fresh again. I start over.

Bedtime.

All the bedroom doors are lined up in a row, with locks on them. They won't let me and Willy sleep in the same room, but at least we're next to each other.

JoEllen unlocks my door and I go in. As soon as she closes the door, I try the knob. It opens. "You forgot to lock me in," I tell her.

She chuckles. "Why would I want to lock you in?" she asks me. "Do you think you're in prison or something?"

Relief washes warm down my insides. I smile back at her. I think it's my first smile of the day.

"I'll be checking on you every twenty minutes during the night," she tells me. "Just in case you need anything."

Nobody in my whole life ever checked on me to see if I needed something. I wonder what other kids need during the night. Books? New sheets? Fruit Roll-ups?

I have to think of something I need so JoEllen will know I'm used to people giving me stuff. Maybe I'll tell her I need another blanket. That's it. When she asks, I'll need another blanket.

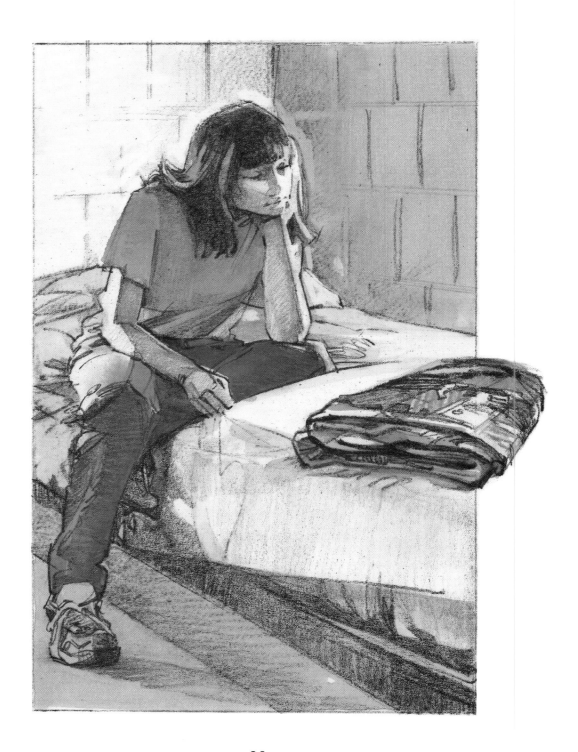

My door shuts by itself, and I sit down on the bed. It has a pillow with a white case on it. I mean really white, not old sweaty gray. I smell it, to be sure. It smells like a laundromat, fresh and sudsy. There's a nice white blanket too.

At the end of the bed, a quilt is folded just right. It's made out of old clothes—jeans and plaid shirts—with red yarn bows tied all over it. Somebody made it, I can tell.

I pretend I know who it was: a lady with straight hair a lot like mine. When her kids go to bed, she works on the quilt and imagines just who will be using it—a very special kid she hasn't met yet.

Oh darn. I guess I have enough blankets. Now I need to need something else.

Maybe I'll say I need the picture I painted. I don't really need my grocery bag. I took out what I wanted, and they put the rest in a locker. Good thing it's in a safe place. It has everything Willy and I own in it. I remember her putting shoes and sweaters and underwear in the bag last night. She said we were going on a long trip. I wondered why she wasn't happy and excited.

Now I know. We sure weren't going to Disney World.

I'm worried they forgot to give Willy his Pooh bear. I go out and knock on his door. "Did they give you your stuff?" I yell.

"Yeah," he calls back.

"You OK?" I ask.

"Yeah."

JoEllen comes down the hall and herds me back to bed. "I'll take care of your brother," she tells me.

My skin gets hard, like a turtle shell. "Nobody takes care of my brother but me," I want to tell her. But I clamp my mouth shut and let my door close.

This time I notice my painting sitting on the desk. What, can that JoEllen woman read minds?

I change into my sweatshirt and sweatpants and clean socks and get into bed. I pile the sheet and blanket and quilt over me and tuck the edges under my legs and arms and neck. You never know what dangerous things could happen in the middle of the night.

"Good night!" I yell to Willy.

"Good night!" he yells back.

JoEllen's footsteps are soft, the TV is quiet. I drift off to sleep. Then *Boom!* I hear a crash. Something flies across the room. *Thump!* Something falls. My mother and her friend are fighting again.

"Are you all right, Darlin'?" I hear someone say. It's not my mom.

I guess I had a nightmare. I'm crammed against the wall, the quilt and blanket wrapped tight. If anyone unwraps me, I think I'll shatter into a million billion pieces.

"What do you need, Honey?" It's JoEllen. Her voice is tender, like she understands my hurting.

I do need something. I feel it like a red wound so deep in me there's no name for the place. I need JoEllen to hug me, like I saw her hug that girl with the ribbons. It hurts to want it, like the sting of salt on a cut.

But what if I say it and she chuckles again, or makes a joke? What if she doesn't hear me, and she just walks out? What if I'm too ugly to hug?

I look up, and JoEllen's waiting to hear what I need. I try, but I just can't say it.

"A glass of water," I whisper. "I need a glass of water."

Sunday. It's been a week now. Willy and I are the only kids left this long. Everybody else has gone to foster homes or group homes or back to their families. We're taking longer because we're staying together. No way anybody's taking my brother from me. Or me from him.

Anyway, the longer we wait, the better the chance that my mom will come to get us. She probably went off and married her friend. But someday they'll run out of money, and she'll come home. Then maybe she'll remember how I kept the house clean and kept Willy quiet and how we never hit her like her friend does.

I decide to tell JoEllen my mother's name. Not mine or Willy's. Only hers. Just in case she's out there looking for us.

In the meantime, we wait. We roller skate in the gym. We play basketball. In ceramics class, I'm making an angel. I make her round cheeks pink. But I scratch marks into her wings, like she's been flying in tornadoes and typhoons. If she's going to be my angel, she better be tough.

Willy and I don't talk much about Mom
leaving. Or about where we're going. He's
happy because they gave him a Bulls
sweatshirt. All day he struts around like
Michael Jordan. But sometimes at night I
hear him through the wall, crying himself to
sleep.

Another Sunday. It's raining, trailing long drops down the window. JoEllen takes us into a room with a police officer. The officer tells us they haven't found her yet, that she probably left the state. They'll start looking farther away.

He tries to smile. But his words tell me what my heart already knew. She's not coming back. She's gone, like a kite whose string snapped.

My body goes hollow, my skin cold. I glance at Willy. I see a tear spill down his cheek. Suddenly I stand up, grab his arm, and yank. "We're leaving!" I shout.

Willy looks at me, scared, the way he does when we open the refrigerator and there's only rotten food in it. Or no food at all.

I've always told him it will be OK. I want to tell him that now. But it's not OK. "We have to get out of here," I say. I drag him toward the door.

Someone loosens my hold on him, and JoEllen leads me down the hall.

29

"You must be angry," JoEllen says as she takes me to a time-out room.

"How do you know?" I shout back. "You don't know anything about me. You don't even know my name!" I want to yell swear words at her, every one I've ever heard. I want to push her until she can't take any more. Why am I being so mean, when she's my favorite person here? Maybe I want her to know I'll be just fine if she leaves. People always leave. And I'm always just fine.

JoEllen closes the door. I act like I want to get out, but I have no place to go. I scream, and she lets me.

I scream the sound of the car door slamming, the way it shot through my heart like a bullet. I scream the tears I held in when Mom told Willy he was a nobody and would be one until the day he died. I scream the way my fists wanted to hit her and hit her and hit her when she'd check out on drugs and I'd have to take care of myself and Willy because she wanted the drugs more than she wanted us. Most of all, I scream at my mother, because even if she stood right in front of me, she would not see me, she would not even know my name.

I don't know if my mouth is against the wall or the floor, but I scream into the concrete until just whimpers come out of me. I don't know how to live without her. How do you live without a mother?

I feel JoEllen's hand, warm on my shoulder. "Will you let me hold you, child?" she asks. Her voice is deep and soft, like a song. She's the only warm thing I know right now.

I nod.

She sits down on the floor next to me and rocks me like I rocked Willy when he was a baby. I don't ever want her to stop. I lay against her, making dents in her arms and her shoulders and her chest. She's like the soft armchair lady—she doesn't mind one bit.

I keep my eyes closed. Tears rise up in me and pour out like hot rain on the cold floor. JoEllen rocks me, and even though there are lots of kids to take care of, she doesn't leave.

Once I open my eyes, just to be sure. It's JoEllen, all right. She's still here.

Finally I'm ready to go back to the TV
room. All the other kids have gone, so Willy's
reading a book by himself, pretending
everything is fine. I know he's been worried
about me, but when we look at each other,
he knows I'm OK. He makes room for me
on the couch.

"Did you ever hear the story about how we
get our names?" JoEllen asks, settling down
beside us.

We shake our heads.

"Way before you were born, an angel—the
Naming Angel—spent days and nights
studying her name books until she came

upon the one name that was perfect for you.
Then she flew down through the stars with
that name written in her heart. She visited
your parents and whispered it in their ears
over and over again, until finally they heard
her. Then she pressed her finger right below
your nose, making a dent. That's her special
seal. It will be there your whole life,
reminding you of who you really are."

Willy and I check for our dents.

"So you see, your name comes from
somewhere far beyond this earth. It's the
spirit of who you are. And nobody has the
power to take it away, you understand?"

I think it's a fairy tale, but I know exactly
what she's saying. I guess I've known it all
along but just forgot.

"Grace," I whisper. "My name is Grace."

JoEllen puts her hand on my head.
"Grace," she says, slow and long, like it has a
taste to it. When she says it, it sounds like
the most beautiful name in the world.
"That's your name all right. I can feel it."

Then she touches Willy. He looks at me for
a signal. "Willy," he tells JoEllen. "William,
for long."

"William," she says. "Willy. If you'd asked
me, I probably would have guessed."

He smiles.

JoEllen begins to hum a quiet song that makes me sleepy. "Grace, Willy," she says, "I will always, always remember you. One of these days you'll be leaving this place, but when you come back to see me—next week or next year or fifty years from now—I'll say, 'It's Grace! It's Willy!' My heart will remember you, no matter how much time goes by."

I'm afraid to trust her words, but they sound so good to me. I close my eyes and drift off with her song.

Author's note

When you have been abused or neglected, the world can feel like a cruel place. It may seem that most people want to hurt you or take advantage of you. It may be hard to trust that anyone will ever love you the way you deserve to be loved. But remember: You were not put on this earth to be mistreated, abused, or deserted. You are here because, like Grace and Willy, you are special. You have precious gifts to share with the rest of the world.

Someday maybe someone like JoEllen will come into your life and care for you without asking anything in return. That person may be a social worker, a teacher, an aunt or uncle, a foster parent.

But in the meantime, you can find the strength and goodness within yourself to make it through. In time, you can discover who you are and learn to use the unique talents you've been given.

Even if the people around you right now don't recognize how wonderful you are, it won't always be that way. Somebody out there somewhere really does know your name.